DAVID M before

enrolling i ered a

love f

clearin 2.

Sinc

Please return/renew this item by the
last date shown to avoid a charge.
Books may also be renewed by phone
and Internet. May not be renewed if
required by another reader.

www.libraries.barnet.gov.uk

NO!

David McPhail

Frances Lincoln
Children's Books

For teachers everywhere.

First published in the USA by Roaring Brook Press
Roaring Book Press is a division of Holtzbrinck Publishing Holdings Limited Partnership
175 Fifth Avenue, New York, New York 10010
All rights reserved

First published in Great Britain in 2011 by
Frances Lincoln Children's Books, 74–77 White Lion Street,
London N1 9PF
www.franceslincoln.com

This paperback edition published in the UK in 2015

A catalogue record for this book is available from the British Library.

ISBN 978-1-84780-713-7

Printed in China

1 3 5 7 9 8 6 4 2

Everyone has the right to be safe and to be treated fairly. But sometimes people can be cruel. And we need to say "No!" when we see things that are wrong, just like the boy in this book.

Amnesty International wants everybody in the world to enjoy all their rights. If people are being hurt and if their rights are being taken away, it is Amnesty who says "No" and works to make things better. We try to tell the world how important rights are.

Lots of our supporters are children.

You can find out more at www.amnesty.org.uk/education

Amnesty International UK
The Human Rights Action Centre
17–25 New Inn Yard
London EC2A 3EA
Tel: 020 7033 1500